# Agatha
## Girl of Mystery

GROSSET & DUNLAP
Published by the Penguin Group
Penguin Group (USA), 375 Hudson Street, New York, New York 10014, USA

USA | Canada | UK | Ireland | Australia | New Zealand | India | South Africa | China
Penguin Books Ltd, Registered Offices: 80 Strand, London WC2R oRL, England

For more information about the Penguin Group visit penguin.com

Original Title: Furto alle Cascate del Niagara
Text by Sir Steve Stevenson
Original cover and illustrations by Stefano Turconi

English language edition copyright © 2013 Penguin Group (USA). Original edition published by Istituto Geografico De Agostini S.p.A., Italy, © 2011 Atlantyca Dreamfarm s.r.l., Italy
International Rights © Atlantyca S.p.A.—via Leopardi 8, 20123 Milano, Italia

foreignrights@atlantyca.it—www.atlantyca.com

Published in 2013 by Grosset & Dunlap, a division of Penguin Young Readers Group, 345 Hudson Street, New York, New York 10014. GROSSET & DUNLAP is a trademark of Penguin Group (USA). Printed in the U.S.A.

Library of Congress Cataloging-in-Publication Data is available.

10 9 8 7 6 5 4 3 2 1

ISBN 978-0-448-46221-9

PEARSON

ALWAYS LEARNING

# Agatha

## Girl of Mystery

## The Heist at Niagara Falls

by Sir Steve Stevenson
illustrated by Stefano Turconi

translated by Siobhan Tracey
adapted by Maya Gold

Grosset & Dunlap
An Imprint of Penguin Group (USA)

# FOURTH MISSION
## Agents

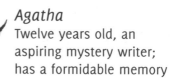

*Agatha*
Twelve years old, an
aspiring mystery writer;
has a formidable memory

*Dash*
Agatha's cousin and student
at the private school Eye
International Detective Academy

### Chandler
Butler and former boxer with impeccable British style

### Watson
Obnoxious Siberian cat with the nose of a bloodhound

### Scarlett
An investigative journalist who's always traveling to remote and unusual places

# DESTINATION

## Niagara Falls, Canada

Toronto

Niagara Falls

# OBJECTIVE

Search the dense and mysterious
Canadian forests for a mastermind jewel
thief, the notorious Ratmusqué.

# For my friend Ermanna

With thanks to the Muskoka Tourism board and the Royal Canadian Mounted Police (the famous "Canadian Mounties") for their reference material, to Gianfranco Calvitti and Davide Morosinotto for their advice on constructing the plot, and to Frida Bifolchetti for her patience (I swear we'll go on vacation next summer!)

# The Investigation Begins...

*H*igh above the streets of London, the orange rays of a spectacular sunset blazed through a tangle of high-tech wires and houseplants into Dashiell Mistery's penthouse atop Baker Palace. The blinding light hid the mess in the living room as its sole occupant dedicated himself to doing what he did best: making an even bigger mess.

Tall and lanky, with dark hair that always flopped over his forehead, fourteen-year-old Dash was multitasking on seven computers at once: rock music blaring from iTunes, friends on chat, a dozen web pages open simultaneously, and— most important of all—installing new software

for his EyeNet, the state-of-the-art device given to students at the detective school he attended.

Nearly hidden by pizza boxes and socks, the precious titanium instrument vibrated with high-speed downloads. Every so often, Dash checked to make sure it was updating smoothly. The new programs would allow him to view microfilm from anywhere in the world, connect wirelessly to other EyeNets, and track the movement of satellites in real time. The aspiring detective couldn't wait to try out these exciting new features on an investigation.

"Watch your back, Sherlock Holmes," he said with a snicker. "Soon I'll be the most famous detective in all of London!"

Satisfied, he put his feet up on the desk and leaned way back, balancing on the rear wheels of his chair. This proved to be a risky move. A moment later, the chair's plastic joints gave way with a *crack*! and Dash fell backward onto

the dusty carpet, dragging a mess of cables, computers, and monitors with him. "What a wipeout!" he groaned, struggling to free himself from the tangle of wires. Fortunately his mother was out, so there were no witnesses . . . He didn't exactly look like the best detective in London!

At that very moment, Dash spotted a silhouette hidden behind the jasmine plants on the terrace. Squinting into the sunset, he could make out a man with a brown peaked cap and a digital camera hiding his face.

The camera flashed ten times in rapid succession, and the mysterious man took off at high speed.

"Hey! Cut it out!" Dash yelled. "Who gave you permission to . . . to—oh no!" His voice caught in his throat. Who would want to immortalize such an embarrassing moment?

There was only one possibility, and it was a doozy: His school must have him under surveillance. And Eye International was staffed by the most elite experts in the field!

Dash jumped up, grabbed his EyeNet, and raced onto the terrace. He looked down the emergency stairs. The man in the brown hat was already a full flight below. There was no time to lose!

"Stay calm," he told himself. "Follow procedure."

Last month, he'd participated in a Tracking and Diversion course taught by Agent MP37,

and had learned the three fundamental rules of shadowing someone:

First rule: Never attract attention.

Second rule: Never lose sight of your target.

Third rule . . .

Um . . . Dash couldn't remember it. "I need to study the manual more," he groaned. "My cousin Agatha can store every detail in her famous memory drawers!"

He raced down the stairs to the floor below, just in time to see the elevator door close. The glowing numbers indicated that it was heading straight to the ground floor.

Dash bit his lip. What was he going to do now?

"The stairs!" he exclaimed.

He raced down fifteen flights at breakneck speed and arrived in the lobby of Baker Palace, panting and sweating. "Did a man with a brown hat and camera go out this way?" he gasped to the doorman.

The elderly man seemed surprised. "Do you mean Mr. Marlowe?" he replied in a quavering voice. "Well, now, I think he just left . . ."

Dash rolled his eyes and shot out the front door like lightning.

He couldn't believe it!

Mr. Marlowe was his whiny neighbor . . . Who would ever have suspected he could be a spy from Eye International? Dash figured he'd better catch up with him fast, tell him his cover was blown, and beg him to delete the embarrassing photos!

Remembering his moves from the tracking class, he scanned the street like a bird of prey and spied a brown hat near a sign for the Underground. Mr. Marlowe walked briskly, checking his watch as though he were late for an appointment. Apparently he had not realized that Dash was hot on his trail.

"I'll get you, you nosy meddler!" growled the boy.

They turned one corner after another, heading toward deserted back streets. Finally Mr. Marlowe slipped into The King's Head, one of the most popular pubs in central London.

Dash stopped to consider his next move. What was that third rule of shadowing? Was he supposed to sneak inside or wait for his target to reemerge?

After a brief hesitation, he decided to stroll slowly past the pub window to check out Mr. Marlowe's whereabouts. Dash spotted him at the bar, conferring with a woman in a blond wig, a floor-length gray coat, and an oversize pair

of dark glasses. The disguise made her features unrecognizable; surely she must be an Eye International agent.

"He must be passing her the camera!" Dash shuddered, remembering his disastrous fall. "I'll be expelled for being a klutz!"

Suddenly the woman looked right at the window, and Dash ducked behind a rusty pipe to avoid being seen. At that precise moment, the third rule of shadowing popped into his mind: Be careful you don't fall into a trap.

"They've lured me here for some reason!" he muttered, running a hand through his hair. "I have to get out right away!"

As he walked down the street, whistling and doing his best to look carefree, Mr. Marlowe and his accomplice came out of the pub. Dash immediately dived into a Dumpster, covering himself with disgusting garbage bags. The possibility that he'd be discovered made him shudder. "No, no, no!" he

begged quietly as he peeked out from under the lid. "I don't want to be expelled!"

Fortunately the Eye International agents disappeared around the corner. Dash gave a sigh of relief and clambered out of the Dumpster.

"Ha! I was put to the test," he rejoiced, wiping slime off his clothes. "But I passed with flying colors!"

He barely had time to finish his sentence when his EyeNet started to beep. Dash thought it must be the Tracking and Diversion teacher calling to congratulate him, but a message lit up on the screen. His face went pale. "An urgent mission at Niagara Falls?!" he hissed. "And here I am, covered with garbage!"

He scraped a banana peel off his sleeve and almost flew down the steps to the Underground. There was just one thing he knew for certain: Without the help of his brilliant cousin Agatha Mistery, he would be lost!

# Unexpected Arrivals and Hasty Departures

*J*ust south of the Thames River in London sat the Mistery Estate, an ancient, lavender-roofed mansion surrounded by a large landscaped garden. Passersby often mistook it for a public park and stopped outside the palatial cast-iron gates to check the hours of operation. Not finding a sign, they would wander off, disappointed, passing between gloomy rows of dark buildings that lined the street.

There didn't even seem to be a doorbell—there was one, of course, but it was cleverly hidden inside a stone column. Mr. and Mrs. Mistery insisted on absolute peace and quiet during their

brief stays in London. They were tireless globe-trotters, always traveling somewhere for work. Now, they were in the wild taiga of Finland, studying the migrations of wild geese and reindeer, so only their twelve-year-old daughter, Agatha, their trusty butler, Chandler, and Watson, the pampered Siberian cat, were at home.

On that cool October day, Agatha had decided to catalog all the books in the family library. She'd started early in the morning and was still roaming around the enormous room with her indispensable notebook. For generations, no one had made a complete inventory of the encyclopedias, novels, and scholarly magazines piled on the shelves.

Agatha was a tireless reader, and every piece of information she found in books was filed away inside her famous memory drawers as something that might be useful to know in an investigation. She got down on her hands and knees, jotting down titles on a low shelf.

Watson glanced at her curiously while playing with a ball of wool, rolling around happily on the Persian carpet.

"It's getting dark in here. Could you please turn on the lights?" the girl asked the butler.

Silent as a shadow, Chandler adjusted the

bow tie of his tuxedo and headed toward the door. He flicked a series of switches, and opulent Bohemian crystal chandeliers flooded the room with light. "Miss Agatha, may I leave to prepare dinner?" he asked, gazing around the library. The grandfather clock ticked past seven. By this time, he was usually standing at the stove in his checkered apron, cooking up something sensational.

Agatha, however, was stroking her small, upturned nose, a sure sign that she was deep in thought.

The jack-of-all-trades at the Mistery Estate cleared his throat and added, "Would you care for smoked salmon?"

Agatha shook her blond curls as though waking up from a daydream. "Excellent choice, Chandler! With your famous lemon-butter sauce, I hope!" she added, smiling. "But before you go . . ."

"Before I go?"

The girl pointed to a high shelf lined with parchment-colored books. To get to them, she would need a ladder. Agatha took off her slippers, gazing at the massive butler. "Could you lift me up there on your shoulders?" she asked.

Without batting an eyelid, Chandler boosted his young mistress up on his rock-hard shoulders. It was a piece of cake for a former champion heavyweight boxer!

"Are you comfortable, Miss Agatha?" he asked politely.

Instead of responding, she raised herself up on tiptoes to grab the books. "Amazing!" she said, flipping through the pages of a medical text. "This will be just the thing for my new story!"

This declaration didn't surprise Chandler in the least.

Like everyone else in the Mistery family, Agatha had chosen an unusual craft. She wanted

to be the world's greatest mystery writer!

She passed the medical textbook down to the butler, who stared dumbfounded at its cover. "Um . . . excuse me, miss . . . ," he said hesitantly.

"What is it, Chandler?"

"Begging your pardon, I wonder just how you intend to read this strange language . . ."

"You mean ancient German?"

Chandler clenched his square jaw and said nothing. Agatha's prodigious talents no longer amazed him, having seen them in use every day: a memory like a steel trap, stunning intuition, attention to detail . . .

"I'm not really fluent," Agatha admitted. "But it doesn't look too hard to learn, once one knows the Latin!"

"I should think not," Chandler said tersely.

Just then, Dash skidded into the library with a jingling of house keys.

"Wh-what's up?" he sputtered when he

spotted the human mountain that was Chandler and Agatha.

"Research and documentation," his cousin replied calmly. "To what do we owe the honor of your visit?"

Dash strode across the carpet, trailing an odor of rotting fish.

As if pulled by a powerful magnet, Watson jumped up and started to sniff him.

The young detective yelped, clutching Chandler's leg in a panic.

Now the mountain was composed of three people and one persistent white cat!

"Call off that beast!" shouted Dash, who lived in terror of Watson's ambushes.

Agatha climbed down and stroked Watson's soft fur. "Dash, you stink!" she exclaimed, holding her nose. "Did you stop for a swim in a garbage dump?"

Dash gave an awkward cough. "Something like that. I hid in a Dumpster . . . Do I really smell that bad?"

"Worse! You need to get into the tub with a whole bottle of scented bubble bath." Agatha laughed. "Let me guess. We're about to go someplace far away, right?"

"You're a mind reader."

"When is our flight?"

"Three hours."

"And where are we going?"

"Niagara Falls."

Agatha flashed a radiant smile. "Perfect! We've never been there!" She nodded at Chandler. "Warm sweaters and raincoats. And we'll have to skip that smoked salmon, I'm afraid."

He nodded in reply and went to pack their suitcases.

"Niagara Falls, you say?" Agatha mused as she and Dash headed into the study. "The American or the Canadian side?"

"I don't really know," confessed Dash.

"If my memory serves me correctly," Agatha said pensively, "the Niagara River flows along the border between the two countries; the western shore is Canadian land, and the eastern is the United States."

"Let me check." Dash consulted the mission data on his high-tech gadget. "Nonstop from London to New York's JFK Airport, then we'll take a domestic flight to Buffalo, an American

city not far from the falls . . ." He raised his eyes. "Your memory drawers are always right," he marveled. "The hotel where we'll stay is in Canada!"

"Excellent," Agatha said, sounding satisfied. "Now we just need to contact a relative in the vicinity."

Without another word, she went to check the family tree, which listed the location, occupation, and relationship of every member of the Mistery family.

"Okay . . . in the Great Lakes region, we have a third cousin named Scarlett Mistery," said Agatha, pointing at the name. "And look, she's a journalist. I bet she'll be really helpful!" She grabbed her phone and quickly punched in the number.

Dash perched on an ottoman, trying to follow the conversation, but Agatha spoke a mile a minute, and he could hear only her.

Moments later, she hung up, looking ecstatic. "Scarlett Mistery writes for a magazine called *Off the Map Tours*, specializing in adventure travel!"

"Another weirdo in the family," sighed the detective-in-training. "Just like you and me."

"She's going to pick us up in Buffalo and take us on a back roads tour of Niagara Falls," Agatha continued. "I can't wait to meet her. She sounds really nice!"

"Did you spill the beans about what we're doing?" Dash asked, worried. He was always stressed at the start of an investigation; he didn't want his school to find out how much he relied on the help of his cousin and extended family.

"What beans could I possibly spill?" she replied. "I don't know anything about the mission yet!"

They were interrupted by Chandler, who dragged in a suitcase on wheels and Watson's carrying case. "So sorry, I wasn't able to find

any warm clothes for young Master Dash," he apologized. "I don't think your wardrobe from Egypt will do."

"It doesn't matter. We're out of time anyway," Agatha said diplomatically.

Dash followed the others into the garage and got into the limousine driven by Chandler. The car sped like a heat-seeking missile through the London traffic.

They arrived at Heathrow Airport in record time, purchased their tickets, and boarded the British Airways Boeing 747 at the last possible minute.

Fortunately business class was almost empty and they were able to talk without prying ears overhearing them.

"Can you tell us about that Dumpster now?" Agatha asked as they buckled their seat belts.

"Um, it's a long story," Dash mumbled.

Agatha shrugged. "And it's a long flight."

Dash sniffed his sleeve with a look of distaste and decided to tell them about Mr. Marlowe, his mysterious accomplice with the blond wig, and the hiding place he had found. "I outsmarted the pros," he said with a grin. "I'm going to ace Tracking and Diversion!"

Watson poked a paw out from inside his cage to snatch a bit of fish off Dash's sweater. He popped it into his mouth, purring with satisfaction.

## Clues in the Sky

"There are a lot of really"—*chomp, chomp*—"strange things about this investigation!" Dash swallowed the last bite of his sandwich, washed it down with a sip of lemonade, and handed the flight attendant his dinner tray.

As she walked up the aisle, she waved her hand in front of her nose. The stench coming from the young detective's clothes was becoming unbearable.

Agatha was used to the embarrassing situations her cousin got himself into, and chose to ignore it. "What kind of strange things?" she asked, drumming her fingers on the armrest.

"Read this," he whispered conspiratorially.

The EyeNet lit up with the detective school's message:

AGENT DM14:

THERE HAS BEEN A THEFT FROM THE OVERLOOK HOTEL AT NIAGARA FALLS. THE VICTIM WISHES NOT TO ADVISE THE POLICE TO AVOID MEDIA ATTENTION. GET TO THE LOCATION, UNCOVER THE CULPRIT, AND RECOVER THE STOLEN GOODS AS SOON AS POSSIBLE.

NOTE: MISSION DETAILS TO BE PROVIDED BY THE HEAD OF SECTOR −5.

Chandler raised an eyebrow in an otherwise stony face. "What does 'sector minus five' mean, Master Dash?"

Dash smiled. "I asked myself the same thing," he said slyly, "and I worked it out with simple reasoning . . ."

Agatha beat him to the punch. "He's talking about the meridian line," she told the butler. "Niagara Falls, like the rest of the eastern region of North America, is in a time zone that is five hours behind London, therefore I imagine the sector is classified as 'minus five.'"

"You haven't lost your touch, cousin!" Dash confirmed grudgingly. "Eye International uses this numbering system for all of its overseas agents!"

"What's so strange, then?" asked Agatha.

"Wait until you hear Minus Five's briefing. You'll see." He grinned.

The boy peered over the seats to make sure that no one was listening, then rummaged through his pockets until he found tiny headsets for his two companions. "These little gizmos connect wirelessly to my EyeNet," he boasted. "Are you ready to try out tomorrow's technology?" He was almost jumping out of his skin with excitement.

Agatha wasn't impressed by high-tech gadgets,

so she took her time. She slipped on the headset, then reached into her purse for her notebook, calmly opening it to a blank page. Only after uncapping her favorite pen did she tell Dash, "All right, we can proceed!"

He obeyed instantaneously, pressing a button.

They heard the crackle of static. Then a distorted voice began to speak.

"*Tchhh* . . . This is Agent RM53, head of . . . *tchhh* . . . sector minus five. At this time I'm engaged in . . . *tchhh* . . . distant investigation. I am requesting backup on my investigation into a significant jewel heist at Niagara Falls. The victim is an Austrian woman, Helga Hofstetter . . . *tchhh* . . . guest at the Overlook Hotel while on a world tour. You'll find a detailed profile attached . . . *tchhh* . . . in the folder . . ."

A long silence followed. When he continued speaking, the agent's words were even more garbled.

"*Tchhh* . . . the line is very bad, I must limit myself to key details. At the time of the theft, between twelve thirty and one thirty p.m., the victim . . . *tchhh* . . . was performing onstage in the banquet hall. When she . . . *tchhh* . . . to her room . . . *tchhh* . . . safe had been emptied. The list of jewels stolen includes . . . *tchhh* . . . *tchhh* . . . *tchhh* . . ."

Agatha signaled to her cousin to turn off the sound and pulled off her headset. "Dash, I can't hear half the words!" she told him. "Isn't there some way to filter the sound?"

"I already did. The distortion is at the source."

"Why? Where was this agent when he placed the call?"

Dash crossed his arms, shaking his head. "What can I say? It's a mystery!"

For once, the clumsiest detective in England was right. It was a truly unusual case!

Agatha put her headset back on, adjusting the

volume and pressing it tightly against her ear to catch every word.

The briefing was riddled with static and frequent interruptions, but she copied down everything she could hear in her notebook. At the end of the recording, her page was filled with question marks. "This will take a lot of work," she noted, chewing the end of her pen. "All right, dear colleagues, where shall we start?"

Chandler and Dash exchanged dubious glances.

"Let's begin with my notes," she decided. "First of all, who's Helga Hofstetter?"

Dash examined the file. "Here's a brief bio, but I could run a search—"

"She's an opera singer," Chandler interrupted. "To be more precise, the world's finest bel canto soprano!"

The two kids turned to look at him and realized that he was flushing bright red.

"I'm one of her biggest fans," confessed the butler, loosening the knot of his bow tie. "I have her complete works on CD in my quarters."

Meanwhile, Dash had downloaded Madame Hofstetter's photo and was smirking at her ample form. "If she doesn't go on a diet, she's going to burst out of that gown on her first high note!" he said sarcastically.

Agatha and Chandler glared at him.

"Okay, no more snarking," Dash said. "Next question, Agatha?"

"What jewels were stolen?" she asked.

Dash clicked on the attachment and gaped at the long list that popped up on his screen.

It was a staggering bounty: three diamond necklaces, a ruby-and-emerald-studded tiara, several gold bracelets, and countless other precious objects.

"Wow!" cried Agatha. "Helga Hofstetter had a fortune in her hotel safe!"

She swiveled around to make sure no one had overheard. Luckily all the other passengers were dozing, lulled by the gentle hum of the engines. Relieved, Agatha looked back down at her notebook. "Next point: the Overlook Hotel. The agent started to give a description of its location and layout, but the recording fuzzed out. Have you got anything on your EyeNet?"

"The hotel opened last year. It has one hundred suites on eight floors, and a world-class concert hall. There's also an open-air promenade that runs the full length of the building, with fabulous views of the falls," Dash read.

"Got a floor plan? Are there any photos?"

"There sure are!"

They leaned in close to study the hotel map on Dash's EyeNet. The concert hall was on the ground floor, and Helga Hofstetter's imperial suite was on the second. It could be reached by a

sweeping circular staircase that curved up from the lobby, but otherwise the upper floors could only be accessed using the panoramic glass elevators.

The Overlook was clearly a luxury hotel, designed to lure wealthy clients. Agatha, however, was not impressed by the ultramodern architecture and deluxe furnishings. She focused instead on features that might prove significant to the investigation. "There is only one entrance, which is secured by alarms," she muttered. "So the thief must have passed through the main entrance—" Interrupting herself, she turned to her cousin. "Did you spot any surveillance cameras? Maybe the thief was caught on film?"

Dash rechecked every inch of the floor plan. "There are loads of security cameras, but they're all mounted on the hotel's exterior," he grumbled. "I wonder why they didn't put any inside the lobby and hallways . . ."

"For privacy," Chandler explained. The Mistery Estate butler had held numerous jobs in the past, one of which was a night guard at fancy London hotels. "There are very strict rules these days; you can't infringe on clients' privacy," he added.

"Of course," said Agatha.

"Well, that doesn't help us at all," muttered her cousin.

"Actually, yes it does!"

"Excuse me? How?"

Agatha flashed him a clever smile. "Agent DM14, have you put all the pieces of this puzzle together?"

"Uh . . . not yet, no! Illuminate me!"

She took a deep breath and explained. "The theft occurred during Helga Hofstetter's recital, between twelve thirty and one thirty p.m., so all we have to do is determine who left the hotel during that time frame."

"But . . . but . . . the thief could have escaped by throwing himself off the balcony into the Niagara River!"

"We aren't in an action film." Agatha laughed. "If my memory serves me correctly, the falls are nearly two hundred feet high. That would be one crazy dive!"

Chandler nodded, and even Watson seemed to confirm Agatha's theory with a little meow.

Agatha sat back and checked her watch.

According to London time, it was 11:30 p.m.

"If there aren't any more files to study," she said with a yawn, "I'm going to take a little nap . . ."

Dash wasn't ready to give up so soon. "We've read all the files, but I'm going to spend all night going over the case," he promised.

Five minutes later, he was snoring soundly.

# Cascading Curiosity

They arrived at New York's JFK Airport in a ferocious thunderstorm. Outside the terminal's windows, flickering coils of white lightning were followed by crashes of thunder.

Everything was gray, including the travelers' faces.

Dash slumped like a zombie in the airport lounge. He never slept well on planes. He had dark circles under his eyes, and his hair was a mess. On top of that, the stench from his clothes had deteriorated beyond belief.

"Don't go out of sight," Agatha recommended. "It's complete pandemonium here!"

"There's a panda here? Where?" Dash didn't sound fully awake.

Chandler took hold of his arm. "Don't worry, Miss Agatha. I'll keep an eye on him!"

"Do you think we should buy him some new clothes before we board our next flight?" she said, concerned. "They might hold him up on bacterial weaponry charges and refuse to let him on the plane . . ."

"It might be for the best." The butler pulled a deodorant spray out of his carry-on bag and spritzed Dash from head to toe.

Dash didn't even notice until he was sprayed in the face. "Wh-what are you doing?" he shrieked.

"Saving the mission, Dash," Agatha said, trying to calm him.

"Oh, right, the mission! Are we at Niagara Falls?"

"Not yet," she replied. "We need to catch our flight to Buffalo first."

During the second leg of the flight, Agatha pored over a Canadian travel guide full of beautiful images of the vast northern wilderness. She always brought books when she went on investigations with Dash; she liked to read up on their destinations. She discovered that Canada is the second-largest country in the world, covered in endless forests and millions of lakes. Most of the population lives in the south, near the United States border, where the climate is milder and industries more prosperous. Only the Inuit community lives in the arctic ice of the Far North.

"Fascinating." Agatha sighed, gently stroking her nose. "What an amazing country . . ."

Chandler looked out the window. "I hope it stops raining. I wouldn't want to meet Helga Hofstetter in soggy clothes." He sighed.

Agatha gave him a wink. "She'll be too charmed to notice the weather."

To their great surprise, the butler's wish was

granted. As they touched down on the runway in Buffalo, the wind blew the clouds apart, letting the sun peek through.

"Are you looking forward to meeting Scarlett?" Agatha asked Dash as they strode toward the exit.

"Scarlett? Who's Scarlett?" From the look of his drooping eyelids, the boy was clearly suffering from jet lag. It seemed to have scrambled his memory.

Agatha led them to the underground parking garage where Scarlett had arranged to meet them. Spotting a cream-and-orange vintage Volkswagen van, she approached it anxiously.

The rear door was wide open, but there was no one inside. Even the driver's seat was empty.

"Scarlett?" called Agatha. "Scarlett Mistery?"

A cowboy hat popped up behind the van. "That's me!" said a silvery voice.

"It's your cousin Agatha!"

Scarlett Mistery closed the tailgate with a thud and rubbed her hands on a bandanna. She stepped forward, grinning, to hug her relatives. "I was oiling the lock on the door," she began. "This old camper's a champ, but it's getting rusty with age!"

She was in her mid twenties, tall and athletic, with smooth blond hair framing a face free of makeup. She looked like an older version of Agatha, right down to the same upturned nose.

She was wearing a pair of flared jeans, a western shirt, and well-worn cowboy boots.

Scarlett gave her young cousin a kiss on the cheek, and was about to kiss to Dash when she took an instinctive step back. "Holy crow!" she exclaimed. "Have you been wrestling catfish or testing deodorants?"

Dash was so embarrassed he couldn't find words. "Oh—oh . . . the Dumpster . . . the plane . . . the spray stuff . . ."

"Come here!" Scarlett ordered. "I've got some clothes just your size and some wet wipes that could degrease a mangy bear!"

Before they'd even finished greeting each other, their distant cousin was herding Dash into the back of her camper to clean up his act.

And she was doing a marvelous job!

Moments later, Dash emerged, smelling human again. The only problem was that he looked like he was dressed for a rodeo.

"Where's your ten-gallon hat and chaps?" Agatha quipped.

"And your Winchester rifle?" teased Chandler.

Dash made a hissing sound like a pot boiling.

Scarlett reached over to shake Chandler's hand and gave Watson a quick scratch under the chin before herding them into the van.

It was an original camper van from the 1970s, overflowing with all sorts of outdoor gear: backpacking tents, inflatable mattresses, hiking boots, flashlights, ropes, an inflatable kayak with paddles, and a trunk full of winter clothes. Scarlett was well equipped for adventuring in the remote places she wrote about.

A copy of *Off the Map Tours* was resting on the dashboard. Agatha was eager to flip through it and read Scarlett's articles, but her older cousin began to speak.

"Have you all got your hearts set on Niagara Falls?" she asked with a hint of disappointment.

"It's kind of a tourist trap, I'm afraid."

"It's an opportunity . . . we . . . can't refuse!" Agatha paused as she tried to think up a good cover for their secret mission. "We've been invited there . . . um . . . by a dear friend of Chandler's!"

The butler looked very uncomfortable.

"A matter of the heart?" asked Scarlett, dropping a wink.

Mortified, Chandler sputtered without saying a word.

"Oh no!" Agatha rescued him. "Madame Hofstetter is an opera star, and Chandler is the president of her fan club!"

Scarlett turned the key in the ignition. "Wow, a celebrity! That's pretty posh!"

"Let's go!" Dash said, flipping his collar up.

Agatha's little white lie had electrified the atmosphere. They all felt like spies.

As the van sped north on the New York State Thruway, the conversation got lively.

Scarlett described her reckless travels through the Grand Canyon, the Rocky Mountains, and the Louisiana bayous. "I once got stranded in a ghost town in west Texas," she told them. "I walked two days and nights to fill up a gas can!"

Agatha gave her an admiring look. "You don't get scared when you're traveling all alone?"

Scarlett laughed. "Can't imagine who would be brave enough to tag along with me when I'm on a job!"

"What do you write about, exactly?"

"Bit of everything," she replied. "Canyoning, hang gliding, off-road destinations . . . In the last issue, for example, I wrote a long article about Area Fifty-one."

Dash, who was fascinated by UFOlogy and the paranormal, perked up at the mention of the top secret military base in the Nevada desert that was rumored to study alien spacecraft. He

grabbed the copy of *Off the Map Tours* from the dashboard.

"Area Fifty-one? That's awesome!" Dash exclaimed, flipping through it. But when he found Scarlett's article, his enthusiasm tumbled down like a house of cards. "But . . . but . . . the headline says the UFO research is a hoax!" he said, disappointed. "Do you really believe that?"

Scarlett laughed. "You bet your boots! Sometimes I do special reports that expose urban legends. Do you really think there are alligators in New York's sewers? That a spaceship really crashed in Roswell, New Mexico, and the Mayans created the Nazca lines to communicate with alien life-forms?"

"I not only think so, I'm sure of it!"

"My dear cousin, the truth is always based on facts and logical explanations!"

These words sent Agatha into rapturous laughter. Not only did she and Scarlett look alike,

they thought alike as well!

Dash crossed his arms. "What about crop circles?" he snorted stubbornly. "Are they a hoax, too?"

He didn't receive a response. Something else had grabbed everyone's attention—a thunderous sound, growing ever more deafening.

"What's happening?" Agatha sounded alarmed.

"Maybe the engine is broken," Chandler hypothesized.

Agatha rolled down her window, shaking her head. "No, it's coming from outside! It sounds like an earthquake!"

The three Londoners stared at Scarlett, who continued to drive calmly alongside the river. "Almost there, kids!" she said with a smile, pointing to the left.

An island separated the water into two parts, and then the fast-moving current suddenly dropped off.

Niagara Falls!

The thundering sound was the roar of the water pouring down from a dizzying height and sending up an immense cloud of mist.

"These are the American Falls, almost one hundred feet high, and that smaller one's nicknamed 'Bridal Veil Falls,'" Scarlett explained.

"But the Canadian Falls, which are also called 'Horseshoe Falls,' are twice as wide and nearly three times as high!"

They sat with their eyes glued to the view, bewitched by the incredible beauty.

"Look at that rainbow!" Dash shouted.

"Magnificent!" agreed Agatha.

Watson jumped onto Chandler's lap and scratched against the window, as if he were trying to catch the shimmering bands of color and swirling mists.

They crossed the Rainbow Bridge, an imposing structure connecting both sides of the Niagara River.

At the far end was a roadblock with the maple leaf Canadian flag flying above it. Showing their British passports, they passed through customs without a hitch. The two cousins watched a boatload of tourists head into the misty spray beneath the Horseshoe Falls. They looked like fleas in a hurricane.

"Kids?" Scarlett urged them. "Where are we going?"

Agatha pulled herself away just long enough to give Scarlett the address of the Overlook Hotel, then turned back to admire the spectacular falls.

"I'm Agent DM14, from Eye International," Dash repeated to the security guard. "I'm conducting an investigation, and I can bring in whatever assistants I choose!"

The man was built like a bison and had planted himself in the doorway of the Overlook Hotel with a grim expression. Even after Dash had shown him his credentials on the EyeNet, he had not moved an inch. "No journalists on the premises. Boss's orders," he insisted. "That magazine woman stays outside!"

What was going on?

Why couldn't they enter the lobby?

It all started with one simple gesture . . .

As they went through the hotel's impressive front doors, Scarlett had pulled her journalist ID card out of her pocket, flashing it at the security guard. She did this out of habit, unaware of the security directives the hotel manager had issued.

It was nearly 12:30. Almost exactly a whole day had passed since the theft from Helga Hofstetter's imperial suite, and Agatha was impatient to get inside and see what went on during that crucial hour.

Scarlett grabbed her hand and pulled her aside. "Did I hear that right? Dash is a . . . detective?" she whispered, incredulous.

"Undercover," Agatha whispered back. "It seems strange to me sometimes, too."

"So where does the singer come in? And Chandler's fan club?"

Agatha searched for the right words. "I had to invent a story because we're on a secret

mission," she apologized. "But there is a singer. Helga Hofstetter, the famous soprano, called Dash's detective academy to report, um . . ." She paused for a moment to glance at the door. Dash was stamping his feet at the impassive security guard, while Chandler tried to calm him down. "At this point, I guess it's pointless to keep hiding the truth."

"I'm all ears," whispered Scarlett, ever more curious.

Agatha leaned against the support railing of the balcony that ran around the outside of the hotel and gave her a detailed account of the stolen jewels.

"You kids are amazing!" said Scarlett, delighted. "You're total Misterys. I should have guessed you weren't here for the view. Can I help with the investigation?"

"You're welcome to, but how?"

"I can collect information from around the

neighborhood," Scarlett proposed. "I'm an investigative journalist, after all. If I find any witnesses, I know how to make them sing!"

Agatha gave her a radiant smile. "Great idea! Let's get started!"

They agreed on the questions that Scarlett should ask and established when they would meet up. Scarlett got to work, and Agatha started toward Dash to let him know what they had organized.

Just as she got to the door, a young FedEx courier hurried out of the hotel, balancing a mountain of envelopes and parcels like a tightrope walker. He slammed right into Agatha with a loud *bang*, knocking her over.

"Excuse me, miss, I didn't see you!" the young man apologized, scrambling to pick up his scattered packages. Agatha helped him gather the envelopes before anything blew into the swirling waters at the edge of the promenade. Dash and

Chandler pitched in, and she quickly filled them
in on her arrangement with Scarlett.

Moments later, the buffalo of a security guard
let out a dissatisfied grunt and allowed the three
Londoners to enter the lobby.

They went straight to the reception desk and asked for Madame Helga Hofstetter.

"With whom do I have the honor of speaking?" asked an eccentrically dressed gentleman who had just crossed the lobby. He wore a gray double-breasted suit with red buttons, a lemon-yellow cravat, and had a neatly trimmed mustache and goatee.

"My name is Rex Cornwell," he continued with a hint of a bow. "I am the owner and manager of the Overlook Hotel."

"I'm Agent DM14 of Eye International," Dash introduced himself with a combative glare. "Is there some problem with me and my trusted assistants?"

Mr. Cornwell stared dubiously at Watson's nose peeping out from Chandler's arms.

"No, detective, you're most welcome here," he said with strained courtesy. "Madame Hofstetter is anxiously waiting for you."

"Excellent. Please accompany us to her room," replied Dash.

Agatha had never seen her cousin act with such determination. He was like a sheriff from an old Western. Maybe it was the boots.

They entered the panoramic elevator, where Chandler combed and re-combed his hair in front of the mirror. Mr. Cornwell escorted them to the singer's door and gave it three delicate knocks.

A flutelike voice trilled from within. "Who is it?"

"Madame, the agents you requested have arrived," announced the manager.

"At last! I shall be there in a second."

They heard heavy footfalls approach the reinforced door. It swung open with a creak that made Mr. Cornwell frown.

"Come in, my dear ones," crooned Helga Hofstetter, wrapped in a massive silk robe. "I

was busy with my curlers and a seaweed wrap. I must look dreadful!"

Chandler stepped forward and gave her a kiss on the hand. "You look as lovely as always, madame," he said gallantly.

"Such a gentleman!" she replied, pleased. "Give me a few moments!" She swept into her bedroom with thudding steps.

Dash could barely restrain a smirk. The famous soprano was the same size and shape as the security bison.

They sat on the sofa, taking in the luxurious surroundings. There were floral cushions and gold damask curtains, with tasteful, expensive furnishings. Mr. Cornwell proudly explained that the imperial suite was the jewel in the hotel's crown, attracting the wealthiest and most discerning clients.

While Dash and Chandler listened politely, Agatha began to wander around the room,

looking for clues. She had no idea what she might find, but the thief must have left some trace of his presence. She stopped in front of the safe, which looked like a heavy steel cube, noticing that it lacked the usual mechanical dial. In its place was an electronic lock.

"Can you tell me a bit about this model?" she asked Mr. Cornwell.

Once again, he began to boast of the state-of-the-art features of his hotel. The safes were resistant to fire and could only be opened by inserting an infallible magnetic card. The code on the card was changed every morning at reception to prevent duplication.

"You call that security?" Agatha sniffed. "All you need is one plastic card to open the safe with no effort at all!"

The manager jumped to his feet. "What are you insinuating?" he cried. "It's the most advanced system on the market. The cards

are recoded daily by two employees, who are carefully screened. If the card is stolen or lost, the sole responsibility lies with the client!"

Agatha refused to let his bluster intimidate her. "You use an electronic system to unlock the rooms as well?"

"Of course!"

"So our thief stole the magnetic card that unlocks the door, and the one that opens the safe," Agatha observed with a wry smile. "And during Madame Hofstetter's performance, he was able to take the jewels with the two swipes."

Mr. Cornwell trembled with rage. "I knew we should call the police," he said to himself. "These idiots are making a fool of me!"

"I beg to differ. Miss Agatha has hit the nail on the head!" said Helga Hofstetter, reappearing in a day dress of flowing blue silk. "I did well to

call Eye International. I turned to them not only because they are a superb detective academy, but because I detest any form of intrusion in my private life."

"Where were the magnetic cards?" Agatha asked her.

"In a drawer in my dressing room," replied the soprano. "I thought they'd be safe there."

"And they were missing after the show?" Agatha asked.

"Yes," Madame Hofstetter answered. "When I got back they were sitting on top of the empty safe."

She sighed, then crossed the room slowly. She sank down onto the couch in a theatrical pose, closing her eyes as though she were about to faint.

Chandler poured a glass of cold water from the minibar and gave it to her. "Don't you feel well, madame?"

"It's merely a light faint," said Madame Hofstetter in a quavering voice. "You can't imagine how fond I was of those jewels."

The butler tried to reassure her with soothing words.

While they waited for the singer to recover, Agatha and Dash went out onto the balcony to consult. The roar of the falls drowned out all other sounds.

"The key to the mystery is to find out who sneaked into her dressing room," Agatha asserted. "Bring up the hotel plans on your EyeNet."

Dash clicked on a map and zoomed in on a small basement room. "The dressing room is under the stage, at the end of the corridor."

"Are these windows?"

"They look more like air vents," he guessed. "The dressing room is below ground level. So that's a dead end."

Agatha gazed at the falls, stroking her nose.

"Are you having one of your brilliant ideas?" joked Dash. "I think we should go have a look at that dressing room . . ."

"That won't be necessary!"

Agatha strode back into the singer's suite and took a seat next to a huge spray of red roses left by an admirer. "Well, then," she said with a smile. "Let me tell you exactly what happened!"

Faced with such confidence, Madame Hofstetter and Mr. Cornwell had to agree.

# The Mouse Who Loved Opera

*A*gatha stunned everyone with her dazzling deductions. "The thief was one of your admirers, Madame Hofstetter," she asserted. "If memory serves me correctly, opera fans often give bunches of flowers and other gifts to artists backstage, am I right?"

Startled, the singer looked at Chandler. "You think the thief is one of my fans?" she stammered.

"We believe so," Agatha replied. "I need you to try to remember exactly what happened in the thirty minutes before and after the show."

Mr. Cornwell banged his fist on the table. "That's enough!" he exclaimed. "I cannot allow

you to treat my guest in this way! Can't you see she's in shock?"

"Do you want us to find the thief or not?" Dash demanded.

The manager tugged at his mustache. "Of course I do, but this child is only confusing things! How could she possibly know that the thief is one of Madame Hofstetter's fans? Where is she getting these extraordinary ideas?"

Agatha folded her hands and leaned forward. "I'm sure of it, because you are a scrupulous manager with an efficient security team!"

"Don't flatter me," he said, sniffing. "Get to the point!"

Agatha glanced at Watson, who was strutting around on the cushions. She took a deep breath and continued. "Listen closely. The performance began at twelve thirty and finished an hour later. All of your staff members were on duty. The audience, of whom there were more than a

hundred, was seated for Madame Hofstetter's performance—"

"So?" Cornwell interrupted her. "What are you getting at?"

"Simple. Am I wrong, or were there a pair of security guards outside her dressing room?"

He threw up his arms in surrender. "I don't know how, but she guessed," he snorted. "Two of my very best staff were there!"

Agatha turned to the singer, who was following the discussion intently. "Nobody entered your dressing room during the concert, madame," she informed her. "So logic tells me that the magnetic cards were stolen earlier, by someone who passed himself off as a fan . . ."

Helga Hofstetter's eyes shone brightly, like headlights in the night. Giving herself a quick round of applause, she got up and flounced around the room as she reenacted the scene. She was so lost in thought that she nearly stepped

on Watson's tail. "I recall that as I finished checking my makeup, four or five fans came backstage," she said. "They brought me a huge bunch of roses, a box of chocolates, a bottle of champagne . . ."

"Would you be able to recognize them?" asked Chandler.

She shook her head, embarrassed. "To be honest, I smiled and signed autographs, but I barely looked at their faces!"

"Well then, we're just chasing our tails," moaned Dash, disappointed.

"Wait!" cried Madame Hofstetter, touching her cheek. "There was a gentleman who kept insisting I sing him an aria from *La Bohème* and just wouldn't go away!"

"I remember him, too," added Mr. Cornwell. "The show was about to start and I had to practically throw him out of the dressing room!"

"Can you describe him?" Agatha pressed.

"Did he have any distinguishing features? Hair, beard, clothes, build?"

"He was a small man, very excited, and so nervous that he dropped his coat . . ."

Dash snapped his fingers. "I'm sure that's our thief!" he exclaimed. "He distracted you for long enough to grab the magnetic cards out of your drawer!"

A shiver of excitement shot through the hotel room. Agatha's intuition had produced a good lead, and everyone pitched in ideas. Helga Hofstetter was able to conjure up some more details about her nervous admirer, and the manager seemed to relax, undoing the buttons on his double-breasted jacket.

Since Madame Hofstetter had not eaten a bite since she discovered the theft, Mr. Cornwell offered to order some delicacies from room service. "Would you prefer beefsteak tartare or seared tuna?" he asked, covering the mouthpiece

of the intercom with his hand. Before they could answer, his face turned purple. "What?" he shouted. "A . . . a mouse . . . in my hotel?"

Everyone turned to follow his gaze and saw Watson curled up on top of the safe, holding something furry between his teeth.

Agatha sprinted over to him. "False alarm." She laughed, removing a scrap of gray fur from her cat's mouth. "This must have come off one of Madame Hofstetter's coats . . ."

"I don't own any furs," the singer replied bluntly. "In fact, I have participated in important campaigns against killing for fur!"

Agatha rolled the scrap between her fingers.

Where had it come from? Watson had been roaming all over the room, but he had discovered his prey near the safe . . .

She returned to the table and showed everyone the strip of grayish-brown fur. "I seem to recall that the Canadian native mammals are moose, bear, and beaver," she said pensively. "Could this be beaver fur?"

Chandler examined it carefully. He had once worked at a natural history museum and knew quite a bit about animal pelts. "Impossible, Miss

Agatha, it's too soft," he said. "Beaver fur is much denser."

"So what sort of animal does it come from?"

Mr. Cornwell gave it a disdainful glance. "Judging by the poor quality, it looks like the common muskrat . . ."

The others looked at him questioningly.

"Muskrat," he repeated. "It's a large rodent that wallows in lakes and rivers and is hunted for its cheap fur."

"Fascinating! But what is it doing here, in Madame Hofstetter's imperial suite, if it's such a worthless piece of fur?" asked Agatha.

"Perhaps it was left by a previous guest," the butler hypothesized.

"I think we can rule that out," Agatha said. "The housekeeping staff vacuumed every inch of this carpet. If they found a piece of somebody's fur coat or anything else that was left by a guest, they'd undoubtedly bring it to the reception desk."

"Exactly," confirmed Mr. Cornwell.

Dash tapped his fingers on the table. "How long are you planning to keep us guessing?" he asked, impatient.

Agatha smiled at him, then turned to Madame Hofstetter. "You told us before that when you returned to your suite, you found the magnetic cards sitting on top of the safe, as though the thief were trying to return them to you—or show off how clever he'd been," she recalled. "I could be wrong, but my instincts tell me he also left this scrap of fur that Watson found!"

"Why would he do that?" asked Chandler.

"Maybe it's his signature," replied Agatha. "I read in the *Manual of Criminology* that some criminals leave behind a personal clue to build up their reputations."

This set off a heated discussion, which only ended when Dash, who was frantically doing research on his EyeNet, called for silence.

"You're right, genius cousin!" he shouted, ecstatic. "Ratmusqué is the nickname of a famous Canadian thief who retired from criminal activity a decade ago. *Rat musqué* is the French term for muskrat. He specialized in jewel thefts and always left a little piece of fur behind to mock the police!" He continued to read off the screen while the others listened intently.

They learned a lot of unusual things about the infamous Ratmusqué. His real name was Rick Moriarty, and he had voluntarily surrendered to police because he just wasn't enjoying his life of crime anymore. He'd been granted his freedom in exchange for his expertise and the return of the stolen goods; he'd never sold or spent anything, but kept all the jewels stashed in his woodshed.

Dash broke off. "Give me a break!" he exclaimed. "The rest of the data is classified top secret. Why would they do that?"

"What does it matter?" said the manager,

rubbing his hands together with satisfaction. "We know who stole madame's jewels . . ."

". . . and it was a mouse who loves opera!" Chandler concluded.

Madame Hofstetter laughed at the butler's joke and embraced him, which made Chandler blush like a baby.

"There's only one problem," said Agatha.

"Right now, all we have is a theory, because the security cameras didn't record anyone leaving the hotel during the concert. How did our thief manage to sneak out the jewels? Did he have an accomplice?"

"Surely there's a list of audience members," Dash said. "Am I right, Mr. Cornwell?"

The manager fiddled nervously with his cravat. "Unfortunately all they had to do was pay for their tickets," he said with regret. "There's no master box office list."

"So now we'll never know the truth!" Dash groaned. "We've lost him forever!"

"Unless . . . ," whispered Agatha.

"Unless?" echoed everyone hopefully.

The girl's face lit up. "Of course!" she cried. "Why didn't I think of it sooner?" She tugged on Dash's sleeve and ordered, "Call Scarlett right now. She'll be able to tell us where to find Ratmusqué—and the stolen jewels!"

## On Ratmusqué's Tail

"Sorry, Agatha, I didn't get any good leads," Scarlett's voice said on the phone.

"Change of plans," replied Agatha, beaming. "Can you by chance see a FedEx office nearby?"

"Yes, there's one just down the street. What do you need?"

"Cozy up to the staff and find out if there was a package sent yesterday morning to a Rick Moriarty."

"Will do. Anything else?"

"Yes, please get the delivery address."

"Okay, little cousin. I'm on it!"

Agatha handed the EyeNet back to Dash.

Only then did she realize that everyone was gaping at her.

"Perhaps you'd like an explanation?" she asked with a shrewd smile.

Everyone nodded in silence, inviting her to speak.

"I put together several pieces of the puzzle," she began, "and realized there was only one way to get the jewels out of the Overlook during the concert: seal them in an envelope, leave it at the front desk, and take advantage of the express post."

"The FedEx guy who knocked you over?" asked Dash.

Agatha nodded. "The very same."

"Indeed, there's a FedEx pickup every day at twelve thirty," confirmed the manager soberly. "Even when there's a matinee concert!"

"But you said the video cameras didn't see anyone come or go!" Dash objected.

"No one suspicious," clarified Mr. Cornwell. "We don't consider hotel staff and service people who come and go daily suspicious. They've been carefully screened!"

Chandler gazed proudly at Agatha and reasoned aloud, "So once the package containing the jewels was taken away by the courier, Ratmusqué just sat down and watched the performance. When it was over, he left with the rest of the audience. No one would have been able to single him out in that crowd!"

Agatha winked. "Genius, right?"

"You're the genius, young lady!" Madame Hofstetter thanked her with a smothering hug in her ample arms. "If you recover my precious jewels, I shall perform a special concert at your home!"

She was so happy that she went out onto the balcony to sing an aria at top volume. Even over the roar of the falls, her high notes rang out.

"I almost—almost—hope this mission fails," Dash whispered to his cousin, turning his head so Chandler wouldn't hear. He was watching the diva, enraptured.

Five minutes later, Scarlett called in with good news. "I've got the address the package was sent to," she announced. "What do we do next?"

"Start the chase!" replied Agatha.

"I was hoping you'd say that." Scarlett sounded delighted.

They said a quick good-bye to Madame Hofstetter and left the hotel. Scarlett was waiting outside in her van, the motor already running. As they buckled their seat belts, a huge, shiny, black SUV pulled up next to them. The window lowered with an electric hum.

"Did you think you were going to take all the credit?" said Mr. Cornwell. "Follow us!"

He used the plural because the grumpy security guard was driving, his hulking

shoulders hunched over the steering wheel. Scarlett shot him a defiant look and stepped on the gas, heading north on the highway.

Her passengers filled her in on their findings. Scarlett paid close attention to every word, but when she heard Ratmusqué's name, her hands shook with excitement. If Chandler hadn't reached out to steady the steering wheel, they would have run right off the road. "The notorious Ratmusqué? The most elusive thief in the world?" she exclaimed. "This will be the scoop of my life!"

Dash gave a slight cough. "Remember, dear cousin, this mission is top secret . . ."

"Well, there goes my Pulitzer Prize!" Scarlett shrugged. "But you should know, I'm so proud to be part of this thrilling adventure!"

She stepped on the gas, handing a road map to Agatha. "Could you please navigate?"

"No problem! Where are we going?"

"You won't believe this, but Rick Moriarty lives in one of Canada's beauty spots: the Muskoka District, also known as the 'land of lakes'!"

Agatha studied the map, stroking her nose with a fingertip. "Found it!" she cried. "I remember the guidebook description. 'A region surrounded by wilderness: pine forests, lakes, windswept islands, and other natural wonders'!"

"Yes, but how far away is it?" Dash asked impatiently. "Give me his address, and I'll plug it into the EyeNet's GPS."

Scarlett did a quick mental calculation. "We're less than two hours from Toronto, and then it's two more to Pine Lake, one of the biggest lakes in Muskoka. We should reach Ratmusqué's cabin just before sunset!"

Her calculations were right on the money.

Mr. Cornwell's black SUV was on their tail, they passed a sign saying WELCOME TO MUSKOKA just

as the sun reached the horizon, painting a vivid orange trail on the lake.

The scene was breathtaking. The hillsides were covered with red maples, golden oaks, and dark pines, like a beautiful landscape painting. Rustic log cabins were scattered along the lakeshore, with docks jutting into the sun-gilded water.

They turned onto a winding back road that skirted the edge of Pine Lake. They hadn't seen anybody for several miles, and dusk was falling fast, so Scarlett sped up.

And so she didn't see the man on horseback . . .

"Scarlett, watch out!" Agatha dropped the map, bracing both hands on the dashboard.

Scarlett slammed on the brakes. The van screeched to a halt with a smell of burned rubber.

Behind them, the SUV's horn blared.

"Are you out of your mind?" Mr. Cornwell

raged, poking his head out of the window. "Who taught you to drive?"

Scarlett didn't respond; she had a worse problem to deal with. The horseback rider she'd nearly hit was wearing the bright red coat of the Royal Canadian Mounted Police!

The officer dismounted, approached the van, and checked Scarlett's license. "You've earned yourself a large fine, Miss Mistery," he said calmly, pulling out his traffic ticket book. Then he added in the same relaxed tone, "And I'll need to impound your vehicle, eh?"

They were practically at the doorstep of Ratmusqué's cabin. This couldn't be happening!

Agatha racked her brains for a solution, but before she could speak, Mr. Cornwell jumped out of his car and started to argue with the Mountie officer.

Agatha winced. The hotel manager was making a big scene. "Did you hear what I said?"

he shouted. "We're tracking a jewel thief! Surely you've heard of the infamous Ratmusqué? If you don't let us through, he might slip through our fingers, and we'll never catch him again!"

The Mountie requested more details. As Mr. Cornwell described the theft, Dash bit his nails, and Scarlett apologized over and over to Chandler and Agatha. Only the hotel security guard stood off to one side, impassively watching the scene from behind his dark glasses.

"Okay, I'll go check this out," the officer said. "If you're telling me lies, I'll be forced to take you all down to the barracks." He got back in the saddle, slipped his gun out of its holster, and took off at a brisk trot.

The cars followed him up to a boat launch next to the lake. The Mountie signaled that they should park there and pointed to a white cottage screened by a thicket of trees. "Wait here in absolute silence," he ordered in an authoritative tone as he urged the horse down the dirt road to the cabin.

As soon as he disappeared behind the trees, Agatha turned to the manager. "Madame Hofstetter requested us not to inform the police," she rebuked him. "Now everybody will know about the theft and Eye International's involvement!"

"Who cares about confidentiality?!" replied Mr. Cornwell vehemently. "What matters is catching the culprit. My hotel's good name is at stake!"

Chandler gave his knuckles a menacing crack, which was echoed by the security guard.

Their standoff was interrupted by Scarlett,

who sat on a wooden bench. "It's all my fault," she said bitterly, pulling off her cowboy hat. "This time I've really blown it . . ."

"So I'm not the only screwup in the family," said Dash, sounding pleased. He regretted his words as soon as he spoke them and patted Scarlett on the shoulder. "Don't be too hard on yourself, cousin. The Mountie is already galloping back!"

The Canadian officer reined in his horse, waving a gold bracelet in the air. "Follow me!" he shouted. "I need backup!"

# Under a Billion Stars

As the group sped down the dirt track, the Mountie told them what had happened at the cottage.

When he knocked on the door, he'd heard suspicious noises coming from inside. Drawing his gun, he had entered just in time to see a figure escape out the window with a package tucked under his arm. He shouted at him to stop, but the figure disappeared like lightning into the thick underbrush.

On the table, the officer spotted some papers and a gold bracelet engraved with the initials H. H.

"Helga Hofstetter," Agatha breathed.

"He left it behind in his hurry to get away," concluded the Mountie. "But this confirms your suspicions."

Dash smiled at Scarlett. No one was thinking about speeding tickets now and, with a bit of luck, they'd catch Ratmusqué soon. She let out a sigh of relief.

"Follow me in," said the officer as he dismounted. "You'll see with your own eyes!"

The first one inside was Mr. Cornwell, who kicked the door open and strode through the room to rifle through the papers on the table. "These are architect's plans for my hotel!" he yelled, enraged. "And look at these photos! That rascal had it all organized, down to the last detail!"

Dash looked at the pictures, which showed the Overlook from every possible angle. Agatha picked up some magazine articles on Madame Hofstetter, and a book of instructions for electronic safes.

They had the hard evidence right in their hands!

Chandler looked out the window, where stars were beginning to show in the sky. "How are we going to catch the thief, Miss Agatha?" he asked doubtfully.

"That's not your problem," stated the Mountie. "I've radioed headquarters in Toronto, and within three hours, these woods will be full of policemen combing the whole area."

"Three hours?" Agatha echoed in shock. "Are you joking? We can't give Ratmusqué that much of a head start!"

"We have a mission to accomplish," protested Dash, crossing his arms.

Mr. Cornwell burst into laughter. "What do you think you can do, kid?" he said, stroking his goatee. "There's nothing but miles of forest out there. Do you think you'll find Ratmusqué by groping around in the dark?"

As Dash complained, Agatha grabbed Scarlett's road map and spread it out on the table. She tapped her nose, trying to concentrate amid all the commotion. During the trip, she'd noticed a place with a curious name near Pine Lake. "Here it is!" she rejoiced, jabbing her finger onto the spot. "I bet Ratmusqué is hiding out here!"

Everyone turned to stare at her. How could she know?

"We'll need some flashlights," she continued. "And hiking boots."

Dash looked at the spot his cousin was pointing at. It was in a park in the rocky hills they had seen from the road. "'Dark-Sky Preserve'?" he read, baffled. "What's that?"

Scarlett's ears pricked up. "Great idea, Agatha!" She nodded. "That would be the ideal place to hide out at night! And the entry trail passes right near here!"

"Could somebody please fill me in?" grumbled Dash.

"The Dark-Sky Preserve is an area protected from the interference of artificial light," said Scarlett. "Astronomers go there to observe the stars without needing big telescopes. It will be completely dark there."

"Come on, you guys!" Agatha urged. "Let's grab what we need from the van and get going!"

They left the cottage and hurried back up the dirt road.

As they prepared for their nocturnal trek into

the hills, they were joined by the Mountie, Mr. Cornwell, and his security goon.

"We're coming with you," announced Mr. Cornwell. "Reinforcements are on the way, but we can't let you go out on your own with that dangerous criminal hanging around."

"We're trained and we're armed," said the officer, touching his holster. The security guard grunted, patting his pocket.

Scarlett looked them up and down. "*Arrgh*," she groaned. "All right, well, three more pairs of eyes might be useful . . ."

Agatha said good-bye to Watson, who was curled up for a nap in his carrying case, and snapped on her flashlight. The others had already started down the path. Scarlett took the lead, feeling confident in her natural surroundings.

They walked stealthily through the forest for a mile or so. The thick foliage and distant hooting of owls made the night seem even spookier.

At one point, they crossed a small stream and the ground became slippery with mud. Scarlett signaled for the group to stop and knelt down, shining her flashlight to illuminate a trail of footprints heading uphill. "We've got you now, Ratmusqué!" she whispered in satisfaction.

"Are you sure these prints belong to our man?" asked Mr. Cornwell.

"They're fresh."

"How fresh?"

"Less than an hour."

Dash shivered, tugging his jacket. "How are we going to find tracks in that rocky terrain up ahead?" He traced the path with his flashlight. "There won't be any mud on those boulders!"

"We'll think of something," Agatha said.

They struggled uphill. The trees gradually thinned out, yielding to lichens and thornbushes. Then the path disappeared into a pile of rubble, and the party was forced to stop.

"Now comes the fun part." Scarlett grinned.

"You know, somehow I don't call this fun," replied Dash.

"Turn off your flashlights for a minute. You'll see quite a show!"

They all obeyed, instinctively raising their eyes to the sky, where a billion bright stars swirled in luminous galaxies. Even the grumpy security guard from the Overlook gaped in wonder. It was a stirring sight.

"Ahem, not to ruin the atmosphere . . . ," Chandler observed, "but I think I see a light!"

He pointed at a massive boulder at the crest of a steep hill about half a mile away.

He was right: There was definitely a flashlight ahead! Its beam swept around in all directions as though the man holding it had lost his way.

"Don't turn your flashlights back on!" warned Scarlett. "If he spots us, he'll turn his off and disappear into the darkness!"

"What's the plan?" asked Mr. Cornwell, crouching close to the ground.

"I propose we surround him," whispered the Mountie. "We'll split into two groups: one to approach from the front, the other to come at him from behind."

They all agreed.

The soft glow of starlight kept them from moving too fast, but the trio of the Mountie officer, Mr. Cornwell, and his goon negotiated the rocky slope skillfully.

Scarlett led Chandler and the kids around the far side of the hill, all the while keeping her eye on the flickering light up above. Dash tripped over roots several times and was covered in scratches, but after a few more minutes they found an ideal hiding spot behind some large rocks near the path. They waited in silence.

Suddenly they heard a gunshot, followed by incomprehensible shouting.

Making his way with his flashlight, Ratmusqué careened down the slope at an incredible pace. Leaping from boulder to boulder, he bypassed the spot where Scarlett's group waited, and zoomed out of sight.

"No way! We lost him!" Dash moaned.

"Follow his flashlight!" said Agatha.

Scarlett and Chandler were the fastest and soon outran the two kids.

Agatha and Dash picked their way carefully over loose gravel and found themselves in a narrow gorge with a foot of water on the bottom. It was so dark they kept losing their balance.

"What now?" asked Dash. "What should we do?"

"Try tracking him with your EyeNet."

Dash sat on a boulder and triggered the infrared to search for heat sources. A circle of light appeared on the screen. "Found him!" he exclaimed, only to correct himself a moment

later. "No, it just flew up into a tree. Must have been an owl . . ."

"There's tons of wild animals in these woods. Try some other function," said Agatha.

"Like what?"

A flash of cleverness lit up her face. "If my memory serves me correctly, you said you had a new function that can align satellites," she said. "If you can direct one to our coordinates, it will probably only see one source of light . . ."

"Ratmusqué's flashlight!"

"Exactly, cousin." Agatha smiled. "Exactly."

# Revelations

On the second try, Dash managed to enter the right coordinates. He waited impatiently, mumbling in frustration. "You're as slow as a Game Boy. Get moving!" he ordered his EyeNet. Then his voice dropped into a trembling whisper. "Agatha? I could be wrong, but I think that flashlight is right behind us . . ."

The two kids turned around quickly and were blinded by a bright beam of light. Dash screamed in fright and the echo bounced off the gorge's rock walls, amplifying it dramatically.

That scream was effectively the end of Ratmusqué's escape.

The thief tried to dodge through the narrow gorge, but Scarlett and Chandler were waiting for him. Quick on his feet, he reversed his direction, but the hotel team had run toward the scream and were blocking his way. The Mountie fired a warning shot into the sky.

Ratmusqué was arrested without a word.

The Mountie handcuffed him and read him his rights in a solemn voice, accompanied by shouts of triumph from the others.

"Great job, kids!" Mr. Cornwell beamed. "Without you, who knows where he would have fled!"

Dash and Agatha were still too dazed to respond. Scarlett and Chandler made their way up the gorge, and the cousins ran over to meet them. "We did it!" Dash cried excitedly. "We caught the uncatchable Ratmusqué!"

There was only one problem. Where had he hidden the package of jewels?

As they made their way back to the cars, Mr. Cornwell showered the prisoner with questions, but Ratmusqué remained stone-faced and mute as a fish.

"He thinks he's smart keeping quiet, but the police will be able to make him talk," Mr. Cornwell said, giving up.

It was after midnight when they arrived back at the cottage, exhausted.

"We should let Madame Hofstetter know," said Agatha.

"Even though we haven't recovered her jewels yet, she'll be relieved that we've captured Ratmusqué," agreed Chandler.

Dash had collapsed onto a deck chair. He took out his EyeNet and scrolled through the contacts, groaning at the slow signal. "*Arrrgh*, the EyeNet is taking forever today!"

Hearing these words, Ratmusqué shifted around in his handcuffs. "RM53," he said.

"Did you say something?" asked Dash, still distracted.

"Shut up!" threatened the guard with the gun.

Agatha's ears pricked up. "RM53? Where have I heard that before?" she said to herself. "Of course! On the plane to New York, we were talking about the head of sector minus five, who gave us the mission briefing . . . But what does Ratmusqué have to do with Agent RM53?"

"What's going on?" asked Scarlett, concerned. "Agatha, you're as pale as a ghost. Are you all right?"

Agatha didn't even hear her cousin. Her brain was working overtime, running through every single thing that had happened since they began

the investigation. When she put all the pieces together and understood the truth, she looked at the faces of everyone present. They had made an enormous mistake!

She sidled over to Chandler and whispered something in his ear. The butler looked startled but managed to keep his composure.

It was time to reveal who really stole Madame Hofstetter's jewels!

"Everyone, your attention please!" announced Agatha, positioning herself in the center of the deck. She realized her voice was trembling with emotion and tried to compose herself.

The Mountie looked at her sympathetically. "Don't be scared, Agatha. There are three more patrolmen on their way," he reassured her.

"Who will they arrest?" she asked.

"That's pretty obvious, isn't it?" The hotel manager sneered. "All the evidence points to Ratmusqué!"

Agatha touched her nose. It was the signal she had agreed on with Chandler.

The ex-boxer balled his huge hands into fists and took out Mr. Cornwell and the Mountie with two well-placed punches. They fell to the ground as if hit by a train.

A split second later, Ratmusqué used his agile feet to knock the gun out of the Mountie's holster, sending it into the lake with a well-placed swift kick.

The security guard was about to jump onto the butler, but Agatha stepped in front of him with her hands raised. "Not so fast," she said calmly. "We've got something to show you."

"What do we have to show him?" Dash looked completely confused.

Agatha winked. "Where the jewels are hidden, dear cousin! Let this man go!"

Scarlett had no clue what was going on, but she trusted Agatha implicitly, so she bent over

the Mountie, retrieving the key to Ratmusqué's handcuffs.

"You'll be our witness, sir," said Agatha to the security guard. "What's your name, by the way?"

"Smith," muttered the man. "Bob Smith."

"Watch this, Mr. Smith!" Agatha approached the Mountie's horse and pulled a FedEx parcel from one of the saddlebags. She returned to the deck and opened it carefully, peeling back layers of Bubble Wrap until something twinkled.

It was chock-full of jewels!

"You see, our two culprits were clever," Agatha explained. "They worked on their plan for months, trying to frame someone who would look guilty because of his criminal past—"

"Back up," interrupted Dash, who still didn't understand how Agatha had discovered the stolen goods. "How did the jewels get out of the safe?"

"Mr. Cornwell stole the magnetic cards from

the dressing room while Madame Hofstetter was making her entrance onstage. Then he took advantage of his freedom of movement around the hotel to steal her jewels, put them in a package, and send it to this address via FedEx."

"Did he leave the scrap of muskrat fur in Madame Hofstetter's room?" asked Chandler.

"Of course," Agatha replied promptly. "Using the excuse that he was going to order us something to eat, he dropped it next to the safe where Watson was playing . . ."

"So where does the Mountie come in?" asked Dash, scratching his head.

Agatha gave a little smile and turned to the guard. "Mr. Smith, did Mr. Cornwell place any cell phone calls as we were approaching the cottage?" she asked.

He thought for a moment. "Yeah, but I got no clue who he was talking to."

"He was calling our friend on horseback, who

we ran into 'by accident' right down the road," confirmed Agatha. "Don't you think that's a strange coincidence?"

The guard nodded, impassive. Scarlett looked impressed.

"The Mountie was in cahoots with Mr. Cornwell from the very beginning," Agatha continued. "The officer was on his way here to retrieve the package he'd mailed, and when his accomplice warned him of our arrival, he came to intercept us. He asked us to wait at the boat launch. When he entered the cottage, he pointed his gun at Ratmusqué, who escaped through the window. Agent RM53 told us in his message that he was engaged in an active mission . . . He'd probably just come back home when he found a mysterious package of jewels in his mailbox and was wondering where they had come from and what he should do. Isn't that right, Agent RM53?"

Ratmusqué, aka Rick Moriarty, took a

step forward, finally able to speak without compromising himself. "I gave up the world of crime years ago, and became the new head of sector minus five for Eye International," he revealed. "But these two thieves couldn't possibly have known that—I'm deep undercover. Bad luck for them!"

Beads of sweat appeared on Dash's forehead. "You . . . you're the agent who gave us the details of the mission?" he asked in astonishment.

"Precisely, colleague." He smiled. "I'm sorry the line was so bad when I sent you the briefing. I was investigating a dogsled hijacking in an Inuit village up near the Arctic Circle! When you landed in New York, I was on my way back to Muskoka by seaplane."

The Mountie and hotel manager stirred; they were regaining consciousness. The security guard, Bob Smith, had one last question. "But why was the cabin covered in clues? The photos, the plans . . ."

"The officer put them there," replied Agatha. "He had all the material needed to frame Ratmusqué in his saddlebags, and he spread it out on the table when Ratmusqué escaped. I bet he thought he'd made a great trade: a package of jewels for a pile of false evidence."

The sound of police sirens came from the distance.

"Are you ready to be our witness, Mr. Smith?" asked Agatha.

"I got to admit, I'm still pretty confused." The guard hesitated. "But you got me convinced, miss. Besides, Mr. Cornwell was a lousy boss . . ."

They all laughed, and Chandler prepared the two culprits for police interrogation, waking the Mountie by throwing a bucket of lake water in his face.

As he scooped up a second bucket, Bob Smith tapped his arm. "Can I?"

Chandler nodded, handing it the security guard.

"This one's for you, boss!" Bob said with a grin, splashing Mr. Cornwell with icy water.

While the two thieves fumed about the meddlers who'd ruined their perfect crime, Ratmusqué took Dash and Agatha out on the dock.

"You two make an unbeatable team!" he congratulated them. "I'll be sure to tell the top

brass at Eye International about the danger I ran into. Without your help, I would have been in real trouble!"

"I just came along for moral support," Agatha said modestly. "All the credit for the happy ending to this investigation goes to Eye International Agent DM14!"

Dash felt a shiver of pride running up his spine. "The top brass?" he whispered. "Thank you so much, Agent RM53!" Then he looked at

the package of jewels, grabbed Agatha by the arms, and jumped up and down with excitement. The whole dock was shaking.

"Victory dance!" Dash shouted, grinning. "We Misterys are an unbeatable team!"

# Mystery Solved...

*S*carlett's van zigzagged between the many lakes of Muskoka. It was early morning, and the slanting sun cast a golden glow over the autumn leaves. A long *V* of Canada geese flew overhead, heading south.

"Can't we stay for a few days of vacation?" begged Dash, basking in the success of their mission. "Muskoka is the most beautiful place I've ever seen!"

"You know what your mother would say," Agatha cautioned him. "If she discovers you're out having fun instead of completing a mission for school, she'll strangle you!"

Dash smirked. "She's so busy shopping that she wouldn't notice if I disappeared!"

"We could make a short stop in Niagara Falls to say good-bye to Madame Hofstetter," Chandler suggested, the tips of his ears flushing pink.

Dash and Agatha grinned.

"Look at you, Romeo!" Dash teased. "I'm sorry to have to remind you, but your . . . umm . . . lady friend flew to Kansas City this morning for the next leg of her tour. Heartbreak hotel."

"Don't be cruel, Dash," Scarlett said with a grin. "Madame Hofstetter promised Agatha that she'd come to the Mistery Estate for a private performance. If I'm in the right hemisphere, I'll do my best to swing by and sit with her fan club . . ."

The butler blushed and scratched Watson's head a little too roughly, eliciting an operatic hiss.

The scenery sped by as they continued to

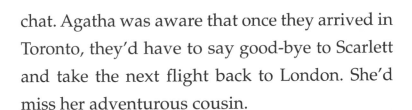

chat. Agatha was aware that once they arrived in Toronto, they'd have to say good-bye to Scarlett and take the next flight back to London. She'd miss her adventurous cousin.

Scarlett and Dash were reliving the highlights of the previous night.

"Chandler's double knockout was amazing!"

"Did you see what a wimp Mr. Cornwell turned out to be?"

"I knew there was something fishy about him. Who wears a cravat?"

"I want to go back to Dark-Sky Preserve!"

After a while, they were all talked out. The magnificent scenery kept unfurling before their eyes, red maples yielding to pines. When the camper van crested a hill with a breathtaking view of the lake, Scarlett pulled over. "What do you say we take a photo to remember this by?" she suggested.

She walked out onto a flat rock and set up

her camera and tripod. As she was adjusting the automatic settings, Dash's EyeNet let out an earsplitting shriek.

"Excuse me, guys, that will be the top brass at my school calling to congratulate me," he gloated, polishing his nails on his jacket. He grabbed the device and answered with a smooth, "Agent DM14 at your service. Who, may I ask, is calling?"

The others watched as his smug expression turned to a cringe.

"Uh, um . . . I assure you that isn't true . . ." He sounded embarrassed.

Who could it be?

Dash ran his hand through his hair. "Why aren't I at home?" he exclaimed. "Uh, because I'm with Agatha. Yes, we're at the Mistery Estate . . . Yes, um, doing homework of course!"

The enigma was getting more interesting. Agatha struggled to suppress a giggle.

"Mr. Marlowe?" he yelled suddenly. "He was the one taking surveillance photos on my terrace! I jumped into a Dumpster to lose him!"

Remembering the stink of the clothes he'd arrived in, the others began laughing harder. Dash covered the EyeNet with one hand.

"What?! You were the one in the pub with the blond wig and sunglasses?" The young detective groaned. "Mom, that's a violation of privacy . . . Okay, yes, we'll deal with this when I get home . . . Soon! Don't ask me when, I'm not done yet!"

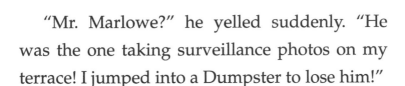

He pulled the EyeNet away from his ear, and everyone could hear his mother's angry shouting.

"Agatha, talk to her, please!" Dash begged.

Agatha took the device and did her best to reassure her aunt. "Dash is staying at my place tonight. I'm helping him with a research assignment on Canada," she lied. "We're watching a great documentary! But tomorrow, Auntie, I'll send him back home, clean and fragrant!"

The voice on the other end sounded polite by the time she hung up.

"So, Dash, the notorious spies taking photos of you were your neighbor and your mom?" Agatha couldn't hold back her guffaws. "Those are some serious criminal masterminds! It's a conspiracy!"

Scarlett and Chandler were laughing so hard they almost fell off the cliff.

Dash had steam coming out of his ears. "What are we waiting for? Can we take this photo already?" he exclaimed. "We've got a plane to catch in Toronto!"

Scarlett adjusted the automatic setting and ran over to join the rest of the group.

A moment later . . .

*Flash*!

The camera immortalized three smiling faces, a white Siberian cat with a big, fluffy tail, and a grumpy, dark-haired teenage boy, hunched over and trying to hide his face under a cowboy hat.

The fame of bumbling Dash Mistery, the young detective who was going to outdo Sherlock Holmes, had spread all the way to Canada!

# Agatha

## Girl of Mystery

Agatha's Next Mystery:
**The Eiffel Tower Incident**

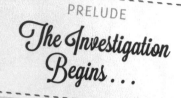

$\mathcal{W}$aking up at eight in the morning for a videoconference on Decoding was not at the top of Dashiell Mistery's wish list. To keep from falling asleep on camera, the Eye International detective student, who was a total night owl, drank can after can of Coke. It gurgled and fizzed in his belly.

But it wasn't just Agent EP34's snooze-inducing lesson that made the young Londoner squirm. From the window of his penthouse apartment, he could see a huge mass of dark clouds rolling toward central London: a blizzard was on the way. Dash peered at the thermometer outside the window and let out a gasp. "No way . . . it's dropped five degrees!"

It was sure to start snowing any minute.

*The Storm of the Year*, the weather websites were calling it. *One of the City's Top Ten*. He had to make his move right away—as soon as that icy snow started to fly, he'd be stuck at home till it was over.

"Um, could be the moment to roll out a few technical difficulties," he mumbled, running a hand through his mop of black hair. "I've been looking forward to a sweet vacation in Paris with my brother, Gaston; why should I let it get ruined before I take off?"

Keeping his eyes fixed on the webcam so none of the other videoconference participants would suspect anything, Dash slowly moved his fingers over the keyboard. He managed to access the settings menu and launched a pirated program with the appropriate name of Electronic Tsunami.

A slight waviness appeared onscreen, followed by a flickering that distorted and fuzzed out his image.

Within moments, the screen looked as though it had been inundated by a devastating tidal wave. The finicky Decoding professor noticed it first, interrupting her lesson. "What's going on, Agent DM14?" she asked, irritated. Then her tone got more urgent. "Agent DM14? Are you still connected?"

Dash began to simulate audio distortion, twisting the foam microphone cover between his fingers. "I'm . . . *FRUSHHHHH* . . . losing . . . *FRUSHHHHH* . . . the signal!" he said, doing his best to sound concerned. "It must be because of the . . . *FRUSHHHH* . . . storm!"

Seconds later, the whole screen went black. He quickly shut down his computer and took out his earbuds. "You're the man, Dash!" he cried, pumping his fists and doing a victory dance.

"No one can fool them like you can!"

He gulped down the last of his Coke, tossed the can on top of the teetering pile on his desk, and pulled on his winter coat, gloves, and hat. His luggage was already packed and waiting for him by the door, but as Dash strode over to grab it, he paused to look at an unusual cell phone hooked up to its charger.

It was his EyeNet, a valuable high-tech gadget distributed by his detective school.

The sleek device was a treasure trove of technological innovations worthy of a master spy, enabling the students of Eye International to carry out their investigative missions all around the world. Most of the time, Dash didn't let it out of his sight.

But he didn't have any assignments to work on right now; he was heading off on a family vacation. He didn't even want to think about school until after the New Year. He stood for a moment, one hand on his EyeNet. Then he made up his mind. "You'll be safe here . . . I wouldn't want to drop you from the top of the Eiffel Tower!"

He put the EyeNet back onto its charger and closed the door, locking it with three different keys. His mother's apartment was directly opposite St. Pancras railway station, where he would board the Chunnel train—the Eurostar that ran through a tunnel under the English Channel. It could reach speeds of more than 180 miles an hour, and it would take just two and a half hours to reach the French capital. It was the kind of technological advance that sent shivers of excitement up Dash's spine.

"I'll get to Gaston's in time for lunch," he gloated as he walked across the street, ignoring the first white flakes dancing through the air. "It's so much better than having to take a plane!"

His thoughts drifted to his beloved cousin

Agatha, who had left for Paris at dawn along with her butler, Chandler, and Watson the cat. They were probably already sitting in Gaston's studio in Paris, and Agatha was probably boring them all silly with her ramblings about French culture and art.

Lost in thought, Dash arrived at St. Pancras in plenty of time. The next train for Paris was leaving in half an hour. As he entered the railway station, he stared at the huge metal arches, the mirrored walkways, and the sleek high-speed trains sitting on the tracks. It looked like a futuristic space port.

"Wow!" he exclaimed, excited.

A voice from behind froze him in his tracks. "Agent DM14? What are you doing here?" Dash didn't have to turn around to know who that squeaky voice belonged to—his Investigation Techniques professor, code named UM60.

What was the professor doing at St. Pancras station? Had he come to punish Dash for his hasty escape from Decoding class?

Flushing red with embarrassment, Dash began to stammer an apology. "Uh, oh, so sorry about the videoconference, I promise it won't ever happen again!"

"I don't know what you're talking about, detective," Agent UM60 replied dryly. "And I don't really care. I have far more important things on my mind!"

The boy let out a sigh of relief. For the first time, he gathered the courage to turn and face his professor. He had to lower his gaze significantly, since Agent UM60 was about half his height.

Since he was used to seeing his professor on a computer screen, Dash had never realized how much the little man looked like a penguin with a bowler hat on his head. He had to stifle a laugh.

"Something wrong, Agent DM14?" the professor asked, bristling.

"Uh, no . . . *hee-hee* . . . I swear."

"Why are you staring at me like that?"

"I see you've got your briefcase with you . . . Are you going somewhere?" asked Dash, doing his best to distract him.

"I should think that was obvious." Agent UM60 sniffed. "I'm taking the next train to Paris. I've got a very important case to solve, detective." He reached up to smooth his waxed mustache.

Dash could hardly contain his laughter. To cover, he grabbed the professor's briefcase. He barely had time to blurt, "Let me help you with that," before he took off like a rocket across the platform.

Unfortunately he hadn't noticed the strong chain from the briefcase to his teacher's wrist.

And so, with a violent jerk and a scream of pain, detective Dashiell Mistery began one of the longest days of his life—and the most dangerous case of his young career.